And a
NOOK GASE
in my
BOOK CASE

There's a WOCKET in my POCKET!

By Dr. Seuss

Random House 🏠 New York

Did you
ever have the feeling
there's a
WASKET
in your
BASKET?

. . . Or a NUREAU
in your BUREAU?

. . . Or a WOSET in your CLOSET?

Sometimes
I feel quite CERTAIN
there's a JERTAIN
in the CURTAIN.

Sometimes
I have the feeling
there's a ZLOCK
behind the CLOCK.

And that ZELF
up on that SHELF!

I have
talked to him
myself.

That's the
kind of house
I live in.

There's a NINK
in the SINK.

And a
ZAMP
in the
LAMP.

And they're
rather nice
. . . I think.

Some of them
are very friendly.

Like the
YOT
in the
POT.

But
that
YOTTLE
in
the
BOTTLE!

Some are friendly.
Some are NOT.

I like the
ZABLE
on the
TABLE.

And the
GHAIR under the CHAIR.

But that BOFA
on the SOFA . . .

Well,
I wish
he wasn't there.

All those NUPBOARDS
in the CUPBOARDS.

They're good fun
to have about.

But that
NOOTH GRUSH
on my
TOOTH BRUSH . . .

Him
I could
do without!

The only one
I'm really scared of
is   that   VUG
under the RUG.

And that QUIMNEY
up the CHIMNEY . . .

I don't like him.
Not at all.

And it makes me sort of nervous
when the ZALL scoots down the HALL.

But the YEPS
on the STEPS—

They're great fun
to have around.

And so are
many, many
other friends
that I have found. . . .

. . . Like the TELLAR
and the NELLAR
and the GELLAR
and the DELLAR
and the BELLAR
and the WELLAR
and the ZELLAR
in the CELLAR.

. . . And the GEELING
on the CEILING . . .

. . . and the ZOWER in my SHOWER . . .

. . . and the ZILLOW
on my PILLOW.

I don't care
if you believe it.
That's the kind of house
I live in.
And I hope
we never leave it.

A
FINDOW
in my
WINDOW